it's about a little bird

Story and Pictures by
Jessica Lange

sourcebooks
jabberwocky

Author's note:
*Hand-tinting black and white photographic images is as old
as the medium itself, beginning with the earliest Daguerreotypes.*

*All the illustrations in the book are photographs I shot and printed in black and white.
I then hand colored them with photo oils. Nothing was done digitally.*

Published by Sourcebooks Jabberwocky, an imprint of Sourcebooks, Inc.
P.O. Box 4410, Naperville, Illinois 60567-4410
(630) 961-3900
Fax: (630) 961-2168
www.jabberwockykids.com

Library of Congress Cataloging-in-Publication data is on file with the publisher.

Source of Production: Worzalla, Stevens Point, WI
Date of Production: August 2013
Run Number: 20983
Printed and bound in the United States.
WOZ 10 9 8 7 6 5 4 3 2 1

For my family.

Adah and Ilse had always been sisters.

They were the best of friends.

When Ilse said, "Adah, let's play!"
 Adah would always play.

Adah and Ilse lived in a city. But their favorite place in the whole world was their grandmother's farm. And one of their favorite people in the whole world was their grandmother.

They called her Mem.

And Mem felt the same way about them. Two of her favorite people in the world were Adah and Ilse. They delighted her always.

They loved to come visit her on the farm. Mem called it *La Petite Ferme*. She spoke French because she had lived in Paris a long while ago when she was a young woman.

Mem had fallen in love with Paris and had been very happy there. She thought it was the most beautiful city on earth. In the evening, after a rain, when all the lights were lit, the whole city shimmered and glistened like jewels. Mem wondered if this was why they called Paris the City of Lights.

Paris was full of gardens and statues. Flower markets and cafes and music in the streets.

And a magnificent river called La Seine that arced like a great ribbon through the middle of the city with many bridges crossing from one bank to the other. One more beautiful than the next.

But Mem's favorite bridge was *Le Pont Neuf*, which she said means "new bridge."

"That's funny," she said, "because it is the oldest bridge in Paris. More than four hundred years old!"

Mem called Adah and Ilse *mes petites choux* and told them it was a good idea to learn French because when they grew up they should go live in Paris like she had.

Mem said a young woman could learn a lot in Paris.

La Petite Ferme means "the little farm," but it should have been called "The Ramshackle Farm." Everything seemed to be falling down. Especially the barn where Adah and Ilse were not allowed to play. It had once been a barn for cows. It was where they came in to be milked. But those days had passed and those cows were gone.

Adah and Ilse were always very busy on the farm. They had many things to do.

There were snakes to tame

and hens to comfort.

The pond in the lower pasture was full of tadpoles. On Easter Sunday they had watched the bullfrogs lay their eggs. Thousands and thousands of them! It was a wonderful thing to see. And when they hatched and started singing at twilight, Mem said, "That bullfrog chorus is positively Wagnerian!"

The girls had chores to do around the farm.

They had baby chicks to tend to.

Their names were Mary the Hen, Sweet Sweet Sweetie-Pie, Trudy, Maude and Ruthie, and Pearly Everlasting.

Jack the dog, who lived on the farm, helped Adah and Ilse look after the chicks. He watched over them all day long and never shirked his duty.

The only thing that still grew on the farm was a field of skunk cabbage. It wasn't much of a crop.

But enough about the farm. That's not what this story is about.

It's about a little bird.

One rainy day, when the girls couldn't play outside and Mem wasn't watching, their curiosity got the better of them and they slipped into the barn. Maybe it was Adah's idea or maybe Ilse's. But most likely they thought of it at the same time. That's how things usually happened.

The rain was beating on the tin roof. It was vast and cavernous inside, like a cathedral. A family of mourning doves cooed from the rafters. A startled barred owl asked "Who cooks for you?"

In the soft half-light it felt very magical and full of mystery.

Adah and Ilse were ready for an adventure. They discovered many treasures laid to rest inside.

There were old pails and milk cans. Iron wagon wheels. Wooden chairs and picture frames. Glass bottles. Blue ones. Green ones. A box of hand-tinted postcards from faraway places.

And a rusted license plate commemorating the 1939 New York World's Fair. Their great-grandmother, Grandma Dodie, had visited the fair that year. They wondered if she had been enchanted by it.

Upstairs in the hay loft was an iron bed. They wondered who had slept in it and what had happened to that person.

But the greatest treasure of all was a beautiful golden birdcage sitting at the far end of the barn. It was incandescent. It glowed and sparkled. What was that doing in this old forgotten barn?

Adah and Ilse ran to the house. They wanted to know all about the splendid birdcage that looked like a castle but was now covered with dust and cobwebs.

Best Ever Banana Bread

2 eggs
1½ cup sugar
little salt
¼ cup oil
¼ cup butter
1¾ cup flour
1 tsp Baking powder
Bananas (1 cup)
1 tsp vanilla
Bake 325 for 1 hour
plus 25 minutes

Mem was in the kitchen baking Grandma Dodie's Best-Ever Banana Bread. She knew the girls must have been exploring the barn. She had seen them coming out.

Isn't that just what children do? she thought.

She was tickled to see how excited they were. So curious and full of wonder.

Mem cut them each a big slice of banana bread hot out of the oven and told them the story of the beautiful golden birdcage and a little bird named Uccellino.

"Before you were born, I was living in Rome. What a wondrous city it is. History everywhere. It is called the Eternal City. There are ancient ruins, crumbling columns, and catacombs laced beneath the ground. Works of art everywhere! Magnificent paintings in every nook and cranny. Fountains built by famous sculptors in all the piazzas."

"But the place I loved the most in Rome was a cemetery where the great poets Keats and Shelley are buried. I would go there just to sit. It was quiet and peaceful. An oasis in that busy city. There were wild cats that lived there and roamed around the graves. I often wondered if they were the guardians of those who rested underground. Or maybe their spirits come back to life to sit for a time in the warm Italian sunshine."

"Well, one day walking home I came upon a shop full of birds. Birds. Every color of the rainbow. All sizes and origins. So many sounds. So many songs! But one, at the front of the shop, was singing his little heart out. It was a canary. Not a bright yellow canary or even a fancy pink canary. Just a plain little rust colored bird. Kind of brown and kind of red. But boy oh boy, could he sing. So I took him home.

"I wish you could have heard him. He had many, many songs and they were all beautiful. He sang all day long. He sang so hard sometimes he fell off his perch. He was a champion.

"I named him Uccello because in Italian that means 'bird.' And I called him Uccellino because that means 'little bird.'

"We lived together in an apartment in Trastevere, which is a neighborhood of Rome. He would follow me around all day, sit on my shoulder, sip water out of my glass, and he would sing for me, filling up the silence. At night he would sleep next to me on my pillow. We were the best of friends."

"But then the time came when I had to leave Rome and go back home. I called to find out what I would have to do to bring a little bird back with me. The people in those offices didn't know a thing. One of them said he would have to be quarantined for six months. That was silly. So I decided to just take him with me. But I knew it had to be a secret.

"When the day came to leave I explained to Uccellino that he had to be very quiet. If he made sound when we went through passport control and customs or on the airplane we would be in big trouble.

"By this time, I spoke enough Italian and he spoke enough English that we understood each other perfectly."

"At the airport I put him in my pocket. It was warm and dark in there and he knew exactly what to do. He was quiet as a mouse. On the airplane I took him out and put him in a little straw basket with food and water. When we got to New York I put him back in my pocket and we went through passport control and customs again. For eight hours he hadn't made a peep! He was a champion."

"But Mem, what about the birdcage?" asked Ilse. "What about that?"

"Oh, the birdcage? Well," replied Mem, "one time I was in Hollywood and I saw that birdcage in an antique shop. The lady in that store told me it had once belonged to John Wayne."

"Who?" Adah and Ilse asked in unison.

"John Wayne. The Duke. He was one of the greatest movie stars of all time. So I bought the birdcage because it was grand enough for my Uccellino. It was a birdcage fit for a champion. If Uccellino had been a movie star he would have been as great as John Wayne. The birdcage was shipped home and that's where Uccellino lived out his days."

"What happened to him, Mem?" Adah asked.

"He sang and sang until he ran out of song. And when he died I buried him under the Buddha out in the garden surrounded by flowers. And that's where he still is."

"Oh Mem. He died. That's so sad. That's a sad, sad story," they said.

"No. He was here and now he's gone. Like Grandma Dodie. Like John Wayne. Like the farmer who worked this land and the cows who came into the barn to be milked. Like the tadpoles someday and the chickens. All of us. We are each here for our own season. So let us rejoice and be glad in it. Like Uccellino did and sing, sing, sing!"

The girls sat quietly for a moment thinking about the story. The rain had stopped. The sun had poked out, turning the sky a soft shade of violet. The air smelled sweet like new mown hay.

Adah and Ilse took their shoes off, ran outside, and danced through the wet clover all the way to the pond to visit the tadpoles. Singing every step of the way.